THE
BIG STINK

Sheila Lavelle

Illustrated by
LISA KOPPER

HEINEMANN:LONDON

To Barrie, whose idea it was

William Heinemann Ltd
10 Upper Grosvenor Street, London W1X 9PA

LONDON · MELBOURNE · TORONTO
JOHANNESBURG · AUCKLAND

First published 1984
Text © Sheila Lavelle 1984
Illustrations © Lisa Kopper 1984

A school pack of BANANAS 1–6
is available from
Heinemann Educational Books
ISBN 0 435 00100 0

434 93023 7
Printed in Italy by
Imago Publishing Ltd

Chapter One

KELLY LOOKED AT his painting and groaned. It was the worst picture he had ever painted, and he knew exactly what Mrs Platt would think of it. A load of rubbish, she would call it. She said the same thing about all Kelly's work.

A bunch of grapes on a yellow dish, it was meant to be. It looked more like a heap of squashed slugs in a bowl of custard. Kelly wasn't much good at art lessons. In fact, he wasn't much good at lessons at all. The only thing Kelly really cared about was getting out onto the sports field on Friday afternoons.

Kelly said a bad word under his breath. The one his dad said sometimes when he bashed his thumb with a hammer. He dipped his biggest brush into thick, black paint and daubed his painting until it was

black all over. The bell rang for dinner-time, and Kelly heaved a sigh of relief.

'And what is that meant to be, Kelly Adams?' said a grim voice. Kelly found himself gazing into the yellow powdered face of Mrs Platt. Mrs Platt was not

Kelly's favourite teacher. She had the worst temper in the world, and she wore so much make-up it was like Polyfilla filling the cracks.

Kelly looked at his black sheet of paper and wanted to giggle.

'It's a black cat,' he said. 'In a cellar. With its eyes shut,' he added. And he grinned round at the rest of the class as they began to snigger.

Mrs Platt tore Kelly's painting from the easel, ripped it into shreds and dropped it into the wastepaper basket.

'I don't think it's at all funny,' she said coldly, and everybody stopped laughing at once. 'I think it's high time you stopped messing about and did some work for a change, Kelly Adams. You will go to the headmaster's study straight after lunch. Clear up now, everybody, please.'

Mr Peel was a kind headmaster and always treated people fairly. But Kelly still couldn't help his knees wobbling a bit when he knocked at the study door a little while later.

'Come in,' a voice said at once, and in Kelly went.

The headmaster sat at a big desk in a

room crowded with books. There were a few old leather armchairs, a faded threadbare carpet on the floor, and the walls were lined with framed photographs of past headmasters and football teams.

Kelly hardly noticed any of it. His eyes were fixed on the row of cups on the shelf behind the headmaster's head. Polished and shining, ready for sports day in two weeks time, they gleamed like treasure. Especially the one in the

middle, the biggest one of all. The Junior Boys' 100 Metres. The one Kelly had made up his mind to win for himself this year.

'Now, Kelly,' Mr Peel began. 'Mrs Platt tells me you're not working very hard at the moment. Is that true?'

Kelly hung his head and poked at a bare patch in the carpet with his toe.

'I dunno,' he muttered. 'I suppose so.'

'I'm afraid all your teachers have complained about the same thing,' the headmaster went on. 'I know sport means more than anything to you, and

we all know how gifted you are. But you mustn't let it become more important than the rest of your lessons. Must you?'

'No, Mr Peel,' said Kelly, feeling his face go red. His school dinner of mince and cabbage made a small gurgling noise in his stomach.

'So you'll try a bit harder at your work, eh?' said Mr Peel kindly. 'Your art lessons as well?'

'Yes, Mr Peel,' promised Kelly, as if he really meant it.

Mr Peel smiled. 'Good,' he said. 'You can start this afternoon. Mrs Platt wants you in the art room at two o'clock.'

Kelly's mouth fell upon.

'Aw. . .sir. . .Mr Peel,' he gasped in dismay. 'It's Friday. It's games on Fridays. I'll miss my training. For the hundred metres.'

'That'll be all, Kelly,' said the

headmaster quietly, and Kelly's heart sank into his plimsolls.

'That Mrs Platt is a horrible old witch,' he said to himself bitterly, as he stumped off down the hall to the playground. 'I'll get even with her one of these days. See if I don't.' And Kelly kicked hard at the wooden fence near the school gate for five whole minutes, which didn't make him feel any better at all.

Chapter Two

KELLY LET HIMSELF in the kitchen door and flung his satchel on the floor in the corner.

'What's for tea, Mam?' he said, peering into the saucepan his mother was stirring on the stove. His mother tasted the contents and added more pepper.

'It's bean casserole,' she said. Kelly made a face.

'I don't want to know what it's been,' he said. 'I want to know what it is now.' He ducked as his mother aimed a jab at him with the wooden spoon. 'Why do we always have to have health food?' he complained. 'The other kids get fish and chips and bacon and eggs and ice cream.'

'The other kids are not going to be Olympic gold medallists,' said Kelly's

mother, ruffling his hair fondly.
'Anyway, it's not ready yet. I want you
to run down to the fish shop for a couple

of kippers for your dad's supper. And pick that satchel up before you go.'

Kelly slouched off down the road, moodily chewing the crust of bread he'd grabbed on the way out. This wasn't turning out to be his day. Not just one lousy painting lesson, but two. Nothing but yucky old bean stew for tea. And worse still, he'd missed his sports practice, all because of that mean old bat, Mrs Platt.

'Mean old bat, Mrs Platt,' chanted Kelly, liking the sound of it. 'Rotten cat, Mrs Platt. Old and fat, Mrs Platt.' Kelly's walk became jaunty. He was beginning to enjoy this little game. If only he could think of a way to get his own back, he thought, racking his brains for an idea.

Just as Kelly was coming out of the fish shop with the parcel of kippers in his hand, it happened. Something about the strong fishy smell of the kippers made him stop suddenly on the pavement as the most amazing, marvellous idea popped out of the blue into his head. Kelly laughed out loud and turned back into the shop.

'Another kipper, please, Mr Wilks,' he said. 'And let's have a big one. The biggest one you've got.'

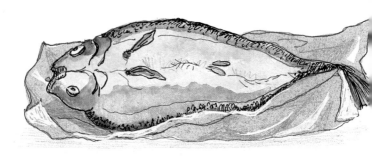

The fishmonger weighed an enormous kipper and wrapped it in brown paper.

'Sixty-five pence,' he said, slapping it on the counter. 'Weighs over half a pound. That'll be a tasty treat for a big lad like you.'

'It's not for me,' said Kelly with a grin. 'It's for my teacher.'

Mr Wilks raised his eyebrows. 'Used to be apples in my day,' he said, shaking his head in wonder.

Kelly didn't hear him. He ran out of the shop, little snorts of laughter escaping from him like puffs of steam from a traction engine.

That kipper had cost Kelly more than a

whole week's pocket money, but it was worth it. He almost flew up the High Street towards home, and turning the corner he ran straight into his friend Tim Connors. Tim was small and red-haired and freckled, and the best footballer in the school.

'What's up, Kelly?' said Tim. 'Won the pools or something, have you?'

'Tim,' said Kelly solemnly. 'Swear you won't tell a soul? Cross your heart and hope to die?'

Tim crossed his heart and hoped to die. And then his eyes grew rounder and rounder as Kelly told him his plan.

Chapter Three

AT EIGHT O'CLOCK on Monday morning Kelly was ready for school. He shovelled down his bowl of muesli, munched his way through four slices of wholemeal toast and honey, and swallowed his vitamin pill with a large glass of orange juice. He collected the brown paper parcel with the kipper in it from the back of the airing cupboard where it had been hidden all weekend.

'Luvverly,' he sighed, putting his nose to the paper. 'Nice and warm and getting a bit high already.'

Kelly stowed the kipper away in his satchel and went into his mother's bedroom, where he found her trying to squeeze into last year's black skirt and making faces at herself in the mirror.

''Bye, Mam,' he said, kissing her
cheek. 'See you later. Cheerio, Dad,' he
added, as his father came out of the
bathroom with a bit of pink toilet paper
stuck to his chin where he had cut
himself shaving.

'Off to school already?' frowned
Kelly's father. 'Bit early, isn't it?'

Kelly mumbled something about
having things to do and scuttled off down
the stairs. He thanked his lucky stars
that they were both too busy getting

ready for work to take much notice of
him.

When Kelly arrived at school there
was nobody about except Mr James, the
deaf old caretaker. He was wheezing his
way around the main hall, opening the
classroom doors with his big master key
that fitted all the locks in the school. He
cackled with laughter when he saw
Kelly.

'Bet you forgot your homework,' he
chuckled. 'Sneaking in to do it before
teacher gets here, eh?' He cackled even
more as Kelly's face turned red, and then
he shuffled away, muttering and
wheezing to himself.

Kelly slipped into the classroom and
went to Mrs Platt's desk at the front of
the room. He unwrapped the big smelly
kipper and pulled a box of large-size
drawing pins from his pocket. Then,

crawling into the dark recess under the desk, Kelly firmly pinned the kipper to the wood on the underside.

Kelly stood up and looked at the desk. The kipper was completely hidden by the carved oak panels all the way around. Even if you put your head in the kneehole and looked underneath, it was too dark to see anything. That kipper might stay there for weeks, months even, before anybody found it. And what a stink it would be making by then!

Kelly did a brief war-dance round the classroom. Then he hurried outside, stuffed the kipper paper in the dustbin,

and went to wash his hands. He found Tim Connors in the boys' cloakroom.

'I've done it, Tim,' he whispered gleefully. And his friend's green eyes sparkled in delight.

That day was one of the best days in Kelly's life. He did no work at all, for all his attention was fixed on Mrs Platt. She kept pausing in the middle of a sentence and sniffing the air in a puzzled sort of way, and Kelly could hardly stop himself from laughing out loud.

When Kelly and Tim left for home at the end of the day, Mrs Platt was emptying every drawer in her desk and sniffing suspiciously at everything she took out. The two boys raced each other home, whooping for joy and throwing their satchels in the air.

'It'll be even better tomorrow,' grinned Kelly. 'Just you wait and see.'

Chapter Four

WHEN KELLY WOKE up on Tuesday morning his head ached, his face burned, he shivered and sweated by turns and his throat felt like sandpaper.

'Looks like flu,' tutted Kelly's mother, tucking the quilt firmly round Kelly's shoulders. 'No school for you today, my lad. I'll go and phone Dr Bennet.'

But Kelly was already struggling out of bed.

'Aw, Mam. I'm all right. Honest,' he croaked, wincing with pain as he tried to swallow. 'I can't stay off school. I don't want to get behind with my work.' His mother stared at him, astonished.

'Why is work so important all of a sudden?' she said. 'Getting fit in time for sports day is what matters at the moment. Do you want to miss your chance of winning that cup?'

'No, Mam,' groaned Kelly, feeling weak at the thought.

'So get back into bed this minute,' said his mother firmly. 'I'll make you a nice hot lemon drink.'

Kelly lay back against the pillows and closed his eyes. What a thing to happen.

After all his planning he was going to be stuck here, missing all the fun. But his mother was right. The important thing was to get better quickly in time for sports day.

When the doctor came a little while later he confirmed that Kelly had flu.

'Lot of it about,' he said briskly, blinking down at Kelly through thick glasses. 'Bed for the rest of the week. Plenty of fluids. Aspirin for the fever.' And he bustled out.

That week seemed to go on for ever. Kelly had books and comics in plenty, and his dad even carried the telly upstairs so he could watch *Bananaman*, but nothing seemed to interest him for long. Day after day he lay there, bored and fed up, and frantic to know what was happening at school.

Kelly found out on Friday, at about

two o'clock in the afternoon. He was
feeling a lot better, sitting at his bedroom
table in his dressing gown and slippers
doing a jigsaw puzzle. Suddenly his
bedroom door opened, and Kelly gave a
cry of delight as the freckled face of Tim
Connors appeared.

'Tim,' he beamed. 'Why aren't you at
school?'

'We've all been sent home,' Tim burst
out, and began to bounce gleefully about
on Kelly's bed. 'Because of the awful

stink. What a shame you missed it all.'
And Kelly's eyes widened as Tim told his
story.

'You could smell it all over the school
by Wednesday,' he said. 'We got moved
to another classroom, so they could make
some tests. First they thought it was a
gas leak, or something. And I didn't half
laugh when they got all the floorboards
up, looking for dead rats. Now they're
talking about a dead body. In the drains.'
Tim rolled about on the bed.

'They've closed the school?' said Kelly
anxiously. 'How long for? What about
sports day?'

'Oh, they'll probably cancel that,'
chortled Tim. 'The whole place is full of
health inspectors and things. Opening
up the drains.'

'What's the smell like now?' said Kelly
in a small voice.

'Putrid,' crowed Tim happily. 'It hits you as soon as you walk in the main door.' He gazed at Kelly admiringly. 'You're a genius, Kelly Adams. You really are.'

Kelly sat by the window for a long time after his friend had gone. He felt a bit scared at the way his joke had turned out. It had all gone a bit too far. He had never meant the whole school to close down.

And what if they had to cancel sports day? Kelly would miss his chance of winning that cup. After all his weeks and weeks of training. He couldn't let that happen.

Kelly began to pace up and down his room, thinking hard. Something had to be done. And soon.

Chapter Five

A FEW MINUTES after midnight that night, when his parents were fast asleep, Kelly got out of bed and dressed in his warmest clothes. Wearing plimsolls so he wouldn't make any noise, and with a black woolly hat pulled down over his ears, he tiptoed silently down the stairs

and out of the house into the street.

The night was pitch black, with no moon or stars to light his way, and Kelly's heart thumped hard in his chest. It was very scary out here all alone in the dark, but he had made up his mind to break into the school and get rid of the kipper. It was the only thing to do.

Kelly ran all the way, glad to find nobody about at this late hour, and when he reached the school all was quiet and still. He crept past the dark and silent caretaker's cottage, and began to make

his way round to the back of the school building, hoping to find a window open somewhere. As he was passing the main door, Kelly stopped and stared in surprise.

The big door stood slightly open, and a faint light gleamed along the tiled floor of the hall. Kelly's mouth went dry. Somebody was inside the school. There were no signs that the lock had been forced. Could it be workmen, doing something to the drains at this time of night?

It must be, decided Kelly, and slid quickly round the door into the hall. At least it solved the problem of how to get in.

As soon as he was inside, Kelly put his hand over his mouth and almost choked. The smell was everywhere, hanging in the air like smoke. It was the most disgusting stink he had ever come across in his whole life. Worse than that dead rat, crawling with maggots, that he and Tim Connors had once found on the rubbish tip.

But all thoughts of the smell went clean out of Kelly's head when he saw that the light was coming from a half-open door at the end of the hall. *Somebody was in the headmaster's study.*

Kelly's legs turned to jelly and he longed to creep away, back to his safe, warm bed. But that wouldn't solve anything. He forced himself along the hall towards the door. Holding his breath, he peeped in.

A tall, skinny boy of about fifteen, in a Spiderman T-shirt and dirty jeans, was standing in front of the fireplace holding an open sack. A short, fat youth with a shaved head and one gold earring was lifting the sports cups one by one from the shelf and putting them carefully in the sack.

'Gerra move on, Grubsy,' hissed the tall one, looking uneasy. 'The old codger might wake up and notice his master key's gone.' He coughed suddenly. 'I can't stand this pong much longer, neither.'

Kelly stepped silently back into the shadows, clenching his fists. They were stealing the sports cups. All of them. Even his cup, the Junior Boys' 100 Metres. He couldn't let them get away with that.

And then Kelly noticed something

that made him stare even harder, his
eyes fixed on the door. The caretaker's
master key. The one these thieves had
stolen and used to get in. *It was still in
the lock.*

The two youths were now starting
towards the door with their bulging sack
and Kelly knew he didn't have a second
to spare. Darting forward he grabbed the
handle and slammed the door shut.
Then, with trembling fingers, he turned
the key in the lock.

He was only just in time. The lock
clicked and Kelly's hair almost stood on
end as the thieves hurled themselves
against the door, yelling and kicking and
pounding with their fists.

'Now to call the cops,' said Kelly
gleefully, rushing across the hall to the
telephone and feeling like Superman.

Chapter Six

KELLY STOOD IN the school hall a little while later, watching the scowling thieves as they were led away by two plain-clothes detectives. A tall police sergeant, with a bushy black moustache, stood over him, making notes in a book. All the policemen had hankies over their noses because of the smell.

'I'll take care of this one,' said the sergeant, and Kelly's knees shook.

The police had arrived in no time at all after Kelly's 999 call. They had been astonished to find that a nine-year-old boy had captured a pair of thieves single-handed.

'They're local kids, of course,' Kelly's policeman told him. 'From the senior school. Knew where the cups were kept.'

'Yes,' said Kelly. 'And they knew the caretaker had a special key that fitted all the doors. That's how they got in.'

'Right,' said the sergeant admiringly. 'And that's how you caught them. Bright little beggar, aren't you? Ever thought of joining the police force?'

'I'm going to be an Olympic gold medallist,' said Kelly, and the sergeant grinned.

'Good for you,' he said. 'Now then.

There are a few questions I want to ask
before I take you home. What was a little
lad like you doing here all on your own,
at this time of night, for one thing? And
what is that horrible smell, for another?'

In the excitement Kelly had forgotten
all about the kipper. He stared up at the
policeman, trying to think of something
to say. There was a long silence.

'It might be best to tell the truth, you
know,' said the policeman gently. And

Kelly found himself pouring out the whole story.

It took quite a long time, but the sergeant listened patiently until Kelly finished. Once or twice he made a funny snorting noise in his hanky that might have been a laugh or a sneeze. Finally he shut his notebook and smiled.

'Sounds like the truth to me,' he said. 'Nobody would be daft enough to make up a tale like that. I think we'll just forget about the whole thing, shall we? I'll take you home before your mam and dad wake up and think you've been kidnapped.'

'Wow, thanks,' said Kelly, his eyes shining. 'But I'd better do something about that kipper before we go.'

'I'll give you a hand,' said the policeman. And together they followed their noses to Kelly's classroom door.

The door had been propped open to let out the smell and the desks had all been stacked in one corner. If the smell in the hall was bad, inside the classroom itself it was unbelievable. It was as if all the rotten, stinking fish in the world had been piled up in one room and sprinkled with pig manure.

Kelly and the policeman dragged apart the heap of desks until they had unearthed Mrs Platt's desk at the bottom. Kelly's eyes streamed, and he was very nearly sick on the floor as he crawled into the space under the desk and unpinned the slimy, rotting mess that had once been a kipper.

'Phaw!' gasped the policeman, holding his nose and handing Kelly a plastic bag from his pocket. 'If that thing was any higher it would need a pilot's licence.'

Kelly sealed the plastic bag and the

policeman opened some of the windows.
The smell was already becoming less
strong, and by Monday it would have all
floated away. The school would open
again and the sports would take place as
planned. Kelly breathed a huge sigh of
relief which somehow turned into a
yawn.

'That'll teach you to roam the streets when you should be in bed, young man,' said the policeman. 'Make sure you never do it again,' and he drove Kelly home, none the worse for his adventure.

They stopped only once on the way, and that was to fling the stinking kipper over the bridge into the river. Kelly had never been so glad to see the last of anything in his whole life.